I Went Walking

Written by Sue Machin Illustrated by Julie Vivas

Omnibus Books

I went walking.

What did you see?

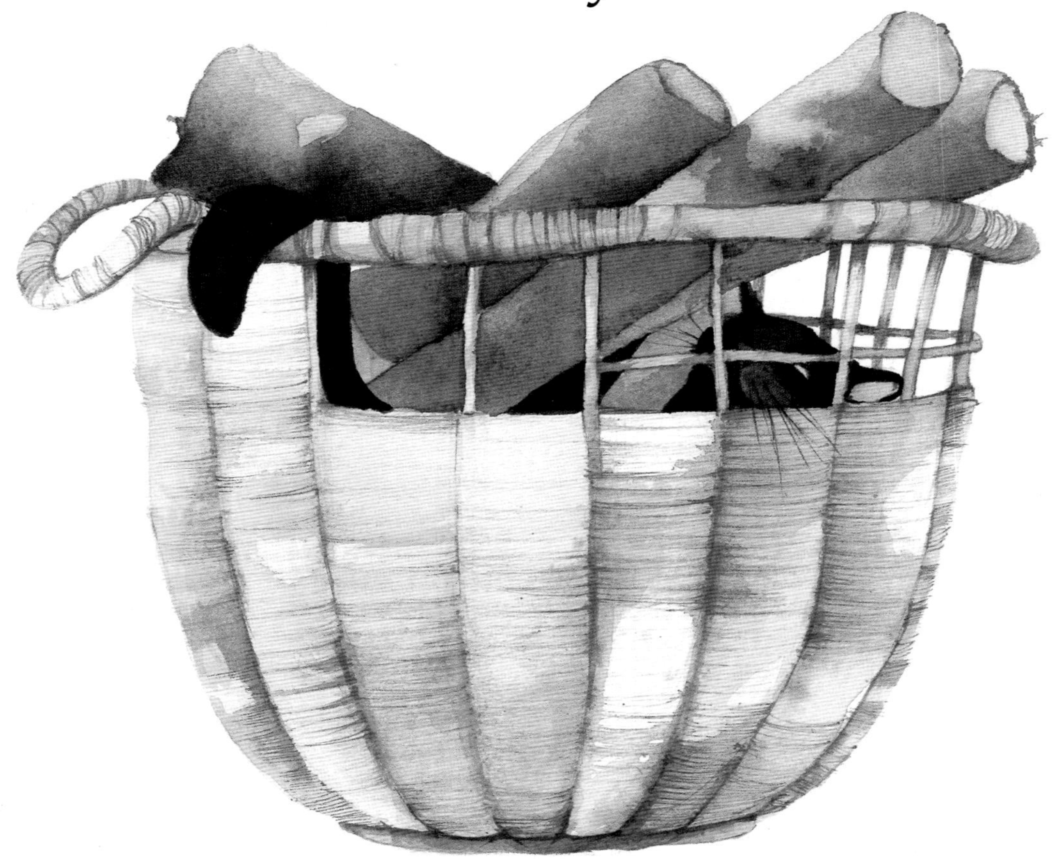

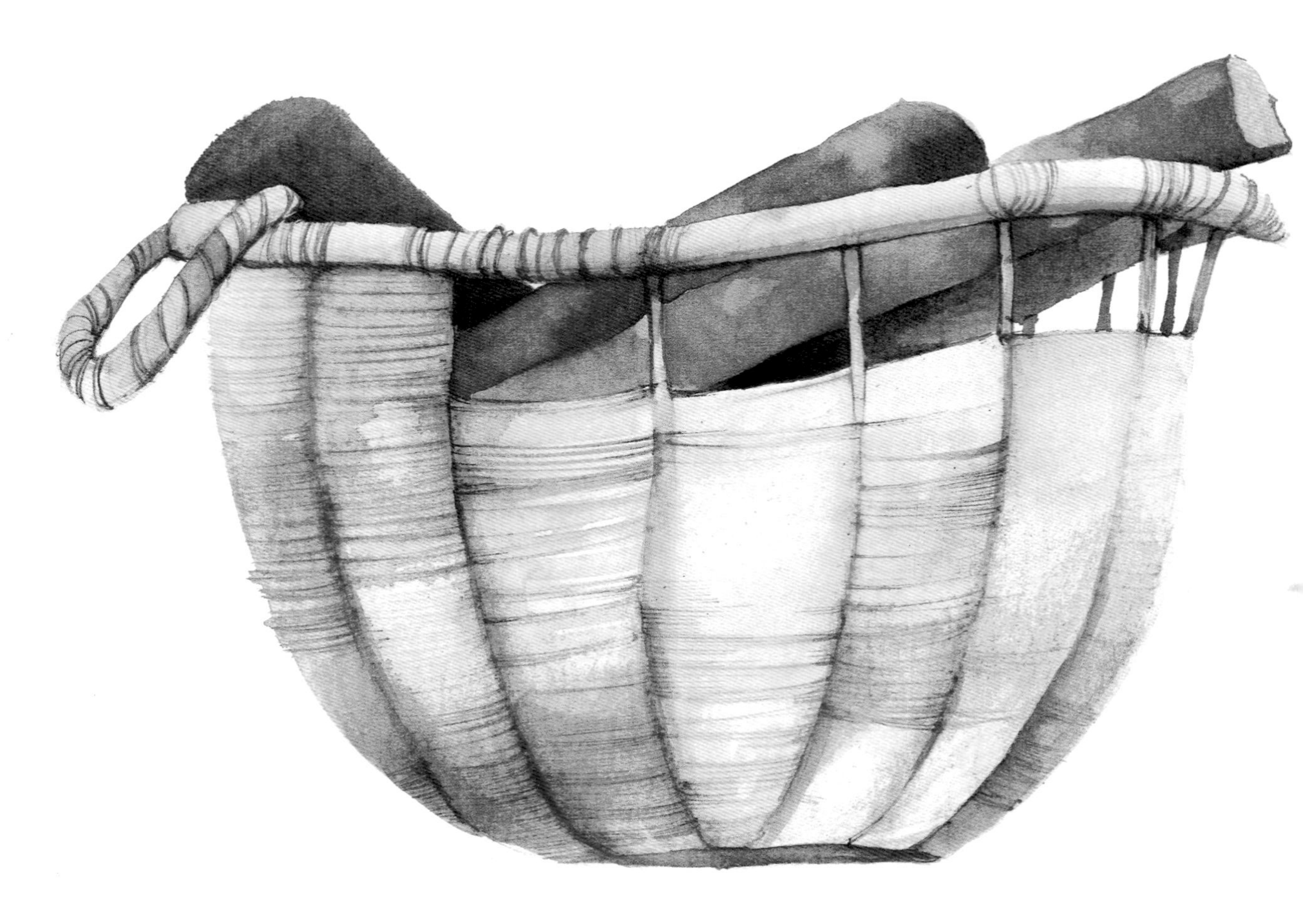

I saw a black cat
Looking at me.

I went walking.

What did you see?

I saw a brown horse
Looking at me.

I went walking.

What did you see?

I saw a red cow
Looking at me.

I went walking.

What did you see?

I saw a green duck
Looking at me.

I went walking.

What did you see?

I saw a pink pig
Looking at me.

I went walking.

What did you see?

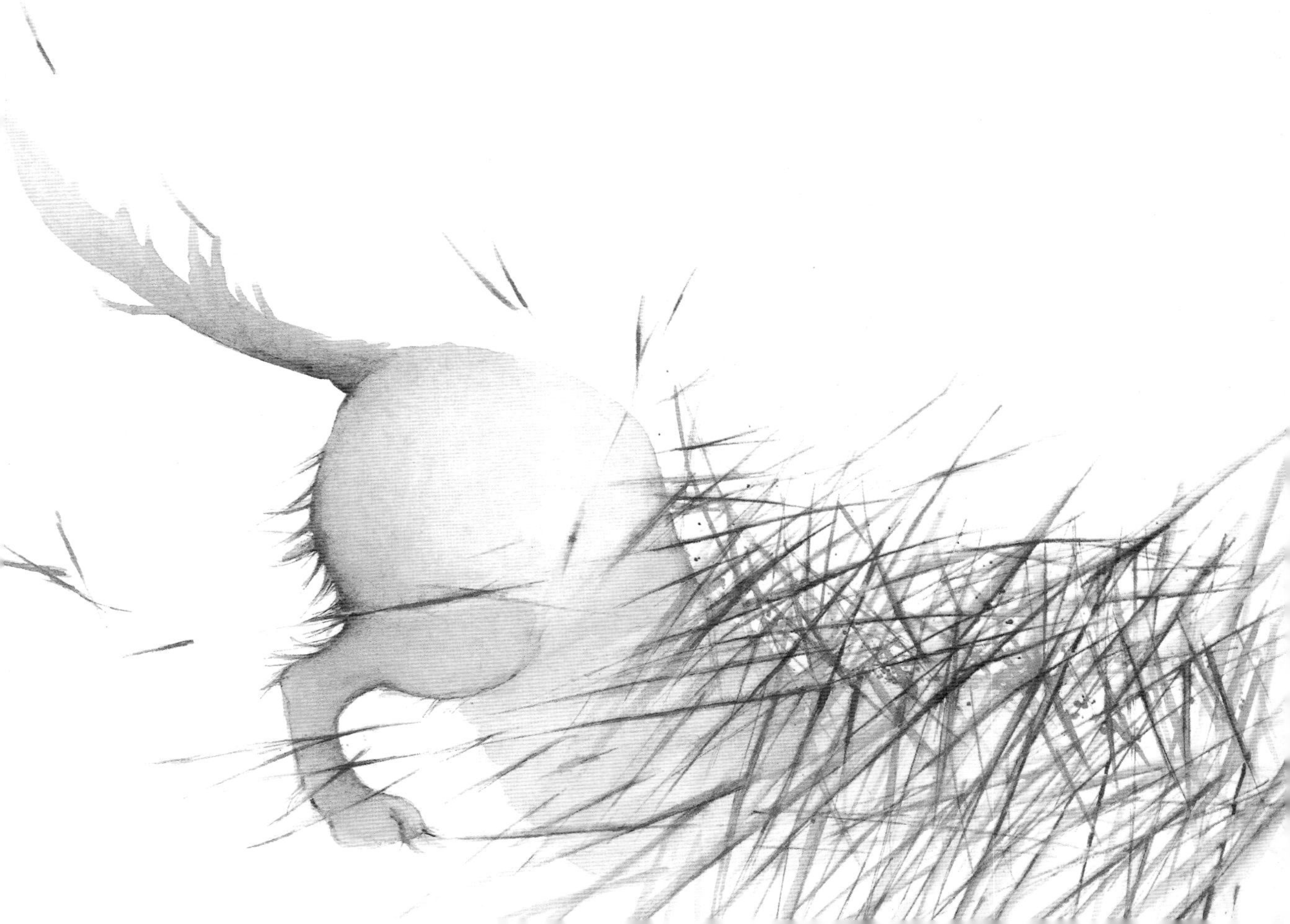

I saw a yellow dog
Looking at me.

I went walking.

What did you see?

I saw a lot of animals
Following me!

Omnibus Books
A.C.N. 000 614 577
52 Fullarton Road, Norwood, South Australia 5067
part of the SCHOLASTIC AUSTRALIA GROUP
Sydney · Auckland · New York · Toronto · London

First published 1989
First published in paperback 1991
Published in this edition 1997

Typeset by Clinton Ellicott, MoBros, Adelaide
Printed in Hong Kong

National Library of Australia Cataloguing-in-Publication entry
Machin, Sue, 1948–
I went walking.
ISBN 1 86291 320 X.
1. Children's poetry, Australian. 2. Animals—Juvenile
poetry. I. Vivas, Julie, 1947– . II. Title. (Series:
Bright stars (Norwood, S. Aust.)).

A821.3